THE PACKAGE

K. BROMBERG

JULIA

"**A**rgh!" The groan rumbles through the elevator seconds after the car jolts to a stop midway between floors three and four. The man who just breezed in like he owns the damn place slams his palm against the brushed metal walls, then clenches his fist on the package in his one hand while he jams repeatedly at the *door open* button and then the *fifteen* button with the other.

Nothing happens.

"Don't bother telling management. It's not like they're going to do anything about it," I mutter from my place in the opposing corner, packages in my hands stacked from my waist up to beneath my chin in the most precarious of balancing acts, and the tracks on my cheeks from the tears I was shedding moments ago hidden by their bulk.

He turns to eye me for the first time, almost as if he didn't even know I was there—not that I'm surprised. I've seen him before. Him and his perfectly styled dark hair and his rough-cut jaw as he breezes in and out of this place day after day like he owns it. I have no clue what floor he works on in this expanse of a building, but I know it's not mine and I know it's the upper half. *The executives' half.* The half where mail girls are nonexistent—good for nothing other than to make crude comments at or completely ignore.

Never anything in the middle of the two.

Ice blue eyes pin mine behind his black framed glasses and a lone eyebrow quirks up. "Come again?" His voice rumbles through the small car, annoyance painting its edges.

And of course his voice is just as sexy as he is. *Just my luck.*

"The elevators are just the tip of the iceberg in this place, if you ask me. Ever since ole McMasters Senior kicked the bucket, this place hasn't been the same. The big wigs on the top floor walk around in their thousand dollar suits and wear watches that cost more than cars. They rule the world from their three hundred and sixty degree view offices while those of us down in the mailroom have to try and sort letters while wearing gloves because the heat is broken and they don't care to fix it. Then there are the bathrooms that rarely work, the budget cuts that have left the cafeteria food not fit for a dog, and the Christmas bonuses? Ha!" I laugh out as the tears threaten again. "Bonuses are only given to the men of this company who pretend to make decisions while everyone around them busts their asses doing the real work."

"Subtlety is your strong suit, I take it?" he asks, turning now to face me. There's something in his voice, a faint lilt in a word I don't quite catch, but the thought fades from my mind when his eyes hold mine. "And what exactly do you mean about Christmas bonuses?"

Unnerved by the intensity of his stare, I glance anywhere but at him. I take in his flannel shirt with the sleeves rolled up to the elbow. The breadth of his shoulders. The rich yet subtle scent of his cologne. What else he's wearing I have no idea because I can't see below my stack of packages.

When I look back up to his eyes as the silence dominates

the space, I recall his finger was pushing the *fifteen* button on the panel.

"Never mind. You're on one of the floors that actually gets a bonus. Forget I said that." I blow out a breath to force my bangs off my face as my heavy coat, this tight space, and my freely running mouth have me getting hot all of a sudden.

Or maybe it's him—hot in all the right ways and I hate that the thought even crosses my mind.

"No." He takes a step closer and my packages wobble in my arms. But he doesn't seem to notice because he's too focused on me. "What did you mean by that?"

The rush of today's events fills my head and hurts my heart so that all the fucks I'd like to give seem to dissipate in that single word, *no*.

I look at him. He's part of the problem. The man who walks into an elevator without a glance backward to the quirky girl from the mailroom whose arms are full. Always too busy trying to save what he seems is the world, one pair of panties at a time.

Jerk.

Take a step back, Jules. Keep your mouth shut. Burning a bridge is never a good thing. Even if some prick like him is the reason you were just fired.

If you finish your deliveries and don't make a scene, Jules, you'll get paid through the end of the week.

The nasally voice of my boss, Barney, and his comment runs through my mind quickly followed by the list of mounting bills I have whose balances I know by heart.

And almost like fate needs to reinforce my luck and lot in life during probably the shittiest of holiday seasons in my life, the elevator harshly jolts up. Yep. You guessed it. That precariously stacked bunch of packages tumbles out of my hands and scatters to the floor accompanied by my strangled cry as I try to steady myself.

Mr. Flannel Shirt emits a noise that's way more sophisticated sounding than mine in reaction.

And just like in those old '80s movies I love, nerves have us rattled so that we both bend over at the same time—a *"Let me help you with that,"* falling from his mouth in that deep rumble—seconds before our heads bonk against one another's.

"Ow!" we both say in unison as we jolt back, but when I step and slip on one of the packages, I fall forward. And before I can faceplant perfectly square into what I'm looking at—the crotch of his dark denim jeans—strong hands grab my shoulders and prevent me from doing just that.

"That package isn't part of your delivery," he murmurs but I can hear the amusement in his tone. "Eyes up here."

Out of breath and more than startled by the bonk to the head and his comment, I look up to see his face mere inches away from mine. Lips. Nose. Eyes.

All of them assault my senses and has me shrugging out of his grasp just as quickly as I pretend not to notice.

"I'm fine. This is fine. We're fine." Each word is a stilted syllable out of my mouth as I silently chastise myself over why I'm so flustered.

"Okay." He draws the word out and narrows his eyes at me with a part-smirk, part-she's-crazy expression on his face. "Your antlers are crooked."

"Antlers?" I ask.

He points to my head. "The ones on your head."

"Oh. Oh!" I immediately reach up for my headband with antler ears and rip them off, feeling more like a kindergartner dressed for the Christmas program while he's the one heading off to the Nutcracker.

"Why'd you take them off? They're cute."

"Cute?" I cough the word out and shake my head. *Did he just really say I'm cute?*

No. He said the antlers are cute.

Not you.

"Yeah. They look cute on you. You should keep them on."

I stare at him blinking more than I probably should, as if I'm trying to process what he just said when I know I heard him just fine. Instead of saying anything, I lower myself as gracefully as I can to the floor so I can start cleaning up the packages.

I have to do something with my hands.

Anything.

Because I'm spending way too much time focusing on him when I don't like guys like him—probably stable. Most likely successful. And definitely thinks he's too good for someone like me.

"Let me help you."

"No!" I all but shout and hold my hand up without looking at him. "I've got it."

"Apparently," he murmurs but leans forward anyway to assist me.

"Just no—I don't—just leave me alone," I snap at him and practically slap his hand away. "You've done enough today."

But when I look up at him and he has a smile on his lips that lights up the freaking elevator in a way an elevator shouldn't light up, I hate him.

On the spot.

For being everything I'm not. For being everything I'll never have. For being the have when I'm the have-not. He's all perfect with what I can assume are his skinny models decorating his side while I'm far from it with reindeer antlers and curves and extra padding that doesn't go away when I shimmy out of the coat I have on.

That's my assumption anyway.

Because men as perfect as him should be illegal.

"Me?" He coughs the word out.

"Yeah. You," I accuse as I rub the top of my head in the same fashion that he is.

"What did I do?"

"You're just"—I point my finger at him and wave it back and forth but verbally fumble over what to say next.

"A shit day?" he asks as if he cares.

"A shit day? *A shit day?*" I screech. "Try going to the bank to pull out cash only to find out that your boyfriend not only decimated your account but then sent you a Dear John letter via text. Oh and the cherry on top of that? My rent is due by the first of the month and now the money to pay it is in his pocket and not mine."

He hisses in mock sympathy. "You sound more angry than upset."

I shake my head feeling more relieved than anything. "The break-up has been coming. The stealing my rent money, not so much."

"Brightside? The prick's no longer in your life."

I glare at him and the cute little smirk he has on his lips. "From the bank, I drove to the train station only to be rear-ended by some asshole on the Expressway." I suck in a deep breath of air and know that he doesn't deserve a single bit of this ire I feel or have a clue of the role he's playing in my catharsis, but I continue anyway. "Then . . . I slip outside on a patch of ice—freaking go down for the count—and I swear to god I still have ice in my panties."

"There are so many comments I can make on that one—frigid, Ice Queen, cold kitty—but I'll keep mum so I can be on my best behavior," he says and I hate the way the playful tone of his voice and the boylike angle to his head makes my body react in the most visceral of ways.

It's the close quarters.

It has to be.

"See? I told you it was your fault," I accuse just to break

my own fascination with the whole of him— the curve of his lips, the strength in his hands, the blue of his eyes, the sexiness of his glasses, the line of his jaw.

His chuckle is low and even. "Your shit day is definitely my fault. I told the prick to empty your accounts and dump you. I told the asshole to rear-end you. And I for sure made that patch of snow freeze to ice just so you'd slip on it." His expression is serious as he fights his grin to try and make me smile. "Whew. Not even a crack of a smile. There must be more then."

"Not only did I get dumped by the asshole—"

"The asshole was the driver, the ex is the prick," he corrects in a professional voice followed with a nod for me to continue.

"Thank you." I roll my eyes. "So not only did I get dumped by the prick, crashed into by the asshole, and have ice in my pants, but when I showed up to work downstairs—mind you I called three times to tell them about my accident—I got a *Merry Fucking Christmas, you're fired.*"

"No!" he gasps playfully but only after my eyes fill with tears and my bottom lip starts to quiver he realizes I'm dead serious. "Shit. I'm sorry."

"It's nothing." I sniff, trying to fight them back but lose the battle as one slips down my cheek. "It's just . . ." I throw my hands up in defeat. "It's Christmas in two days. All I wanted from Alex—"

"Alex?"

"The prick," I hiccup over the word, fighting back the downpour of emotions that are threatening to spill out. "All I wanted was to feel special. My only wish was for dinner at Tavern on the Green so I could pretend to feel like I belonged here in this city. Like I was one of those who work on the fifteenth floor . . . and—and—never mind. Just . . . oh my god." I bury my face in my hands as embarrassment hits me squarely in the solar plexus.

"What?" he asks, concern in his voice although I'm certain he's more worried about being trapped for much longer in an elevator with Crazy-Emotional-Mail-Room-Girl.

"I'm sorry." I shake my head and pretend like I don't have tear tracks on my cheeks. "Here I am trapped in an elevator spilling my heart out to some guy who doesn't care in the least like some idiot. I'll just collect my packages and be on my merry way."

I scramble to swipe a tear away with one hand while picking up a small box and stack it with another. Swipe. Stack. Swipe. Stack.

"There's one problem," he says after a few moments and has my attention pulling back up to him.

"What's that?"

"There's no merry way for you to go on. We're trapped in an elevator. We're not going anywhere for a while."

"Then we should stop talking. Right? We should conserve the air." Panic hits me out of the blue. Why didn't I think of that before I just went and sucked up all the oxygen with my blabber-fest. "*Oh crap.*"

But he just stands there and stares down at me with the slightest bit of amusement etched in the lines of his face. "What's your name?"

"Jules."

"Jules?"

"Julia Jilliland."

"Wow," he laughs the word out. "That's a mouthful. Nice to meet you, Jules Jilliland of the mail room"—he sticks his hand out to shake mine and when our hands touch, his voice falters for a second—"I'm—uh—I'm—"

We both jump to our feet as the phone on the panel beside him rings harshly. His laugh is what resonates though

—that and the warmth in my hand where his was moments before—when he brings the receiver to his ear.

"Should we be concerned that it took you this long to call? Cell service is shit in here so we're depending on you to save our asses," he says to whoever it is on the other end of the line with a laugh.

And I smile.

I hate that I do.

His nonchalance is as sexy as it is irritating. And of course now that he's turned to face the panel, I get a more than ample look at his backside. A backside, I might add, that is complimented by a very fine ass.

It's not like I expected any less. He's got the glasses that are sexy as hell. The rolled up cuffs that show strong forearms. Eyes that question and suggest and are hotter than hell. A sense of humor that I pretend I don't find funny. The nice ass . . . I mean, of course I get trapped in an elevator with perfection like him.

"Thank you. Yes, we're fine. There could be worse ways to pass the time days before Christmas," he jokes. "Can I assume we'll be out before then? Christmas, that is? Because if not, Jules and I should probably start panicking more." He nods when the person on the other end of the line says something and laughs. "That and we'd definitely need some Red Vines dropped down through the hatch." Another chuckle. Another nod. "Thank you."

When he hangs up the phone, he turns so that his shoulders lean against the wall, his hands are on the rail that lines the car, one ankle is crossed over the other, and his eyes right on me. "They're working on it. They said it shouldn't take much longer."

"*Red Vines?*"

"Sustenance," he says with a wink.

"Then you should have asked for Twizzlers."

"Seriously? I'm trapped in an elevator with someone who loves Twizzlers? Just means more for me then. Hey, are you sure that wasn't why you were fired because loving Twizzlers is one of those things that is hard to overlook."

"Hardy-har-har," I say with a shake of my head.

"Did you actually just say hardy-har-har?" He laughs.

"Yes. It's been a shit day. I'm allowed to say whatever the hell I want." But I smile and it feels so damn good after the day I've had.

I squat back down as gracefully as I can in my skirt to continue picking up the vomit of brown parcels that pretty much look identical at my feet. The packages that are supposed to be my ticket to making a difference in this place. My first step in working my way up the corporate ladder that apparently ends at the first rung for me.

"You know I could help you, right? It doesn't make you any less capable if I do."

"Mmm." It's all I say knowing I'm mad at him for not helping me and at the same time acknowledging I don't want his help.

Or rather, maybe it's that I don't want his help because the more he talks, the more he makes me laugh, the more I'm forgetting he's one of those who work here I'm not supposed to like.

The more I can pretend that he's not as attractive as he really is.

"*Mmm?*" He repeats the sound I made back at me. "Is that a yes, you'll accept my help now, or a no, you think I'm a bastard simply because I have a dick, type of sound?"

My eyes flash up to meet his from where he stands and amusement lights up his eyes, but his face remains completely impassive all but for the muscle feathering in his jaw.

And of course, now my mind is fixated on his dick.

"Cute." I force the word out, just like I force myself to stop thinking of his particular *package*.

He shrugs. "You're the one who was going to chew me out for helping. I'd rather keep my hands firmly attached than risk one being ripped off." He holds his hands out and wiggles his fingers. "They do come in handy."

"I've got it," I huff out, mad at myself for not letting him help before the words are even out. "Thank you for offering though," I add, more than willing to admit my bad mood isn't his fault.

"You're welcome."

The silence returns followed by a clank somewhere above us that has me looking up at the ceiling and catching his eye.

"You can stop staring at me now," I mutter as I grab another package and place it in the pile.

"I haven't seen you around. Are you new to the company?"

"Nope. Worked here for ten months."

"No shit."

"Not surprising really."

"Why do I feel like you're constantly talking in riddles?"

"What floor were you heading to?" I ask, needing to jolt myself back to reality and stop this school girl crush that is blossoming.

"Fifteen."

I snort. "Exactly."

Mail girls don't mix with executives here at Garters & Lace. That's the first rule you learn when you start working here.

He squats down on his haunches so that he's eye level with me. That gaze causing my pulse to race and the space around us to feel like it's shrinking. "There's those riddles again, Jules."

2

ARCHER

"You have the most peculiar eyes?" I murmur and earn a startled shake of her head.

And they are peculiar as they narrow and look at me. Dark blue outlines her irises while a light gray fills their center. They are loaded with about as much distrust as there is curiosity.

She snorts.

It's fucking adorable.

Almost as adorable as her in her black Doc Martens and sparkly tights beneath her peacoat. Not someone I would look twice at on a normal day—*call me a dick* for the admission—but there is something about her, something about the look in her eyes and the sarcasm in her voice that has me taking a second look.

Other than her reindeer antlers now thrown to the ground beside her packages.

Like the chocolate colored hair that is pulled up in a top knot. The full lips painted a pale pink and her eyes . . . they're almost too big for her face but they are so stunning framed with thick, dark lashes that they pull you in.

"I'm not talking in riddles, you're just not someone who notices a girl like me."

I open my mouth to refute her but know damn well she's right . . . and for the first time I hate it. But more than that, I hate hearing her opinion about Garters & Lace. About working here.

"I beg to differ," I assert. "I know quite a lot about you. Prick. Asshole. Shitty ice. Fucking boss. Twizzlers. See? I know a lot more about you than you think I do."

Don't smile, Jules.

I dare you not to.

Ah, there it is. Those lips of hers turn up at the corners and soften the sadness on her face.

Her cheeks flush pink as she starts to pull her jacket off like claustrophobia has just hit. And, hell yes, I should be worried about her sudden moment of panic but I'm too busy noticing the roadmap of curves she just unearthed beneath the shapeless coat.

Wow.

One word. That's all I have time to think as I take in the swell of her tits and the curve of her hips beneath the form fitting crazy Christmas sweater that makes me want to say ho-ho-ho.

Wow.

"Only because you're forced to." The hostility in her voice pulls me from staring too long and before I can ask what she means, the elevator car jerks.

We both jolt in reaction as she falls forward onto a package before grabbing onto the railing to catch her fall.

"Jesus," she blurts as panic flickers through her eyes, her knuckles white as they grip tight.

"He *is* the reason for the season," I say, trying to calm her some, but get a glare instead. And I hold it, so very curious about Jules Jilliland and her Docs. "Hey, if you've been fired, why are you still carrying packages?"

She grits her teeth and temper fires in her eyes. If you'd asked me five minutes ago if she was sexy, I would have told you she's more the adorable type—button nose, full lips, innocent eyes—but that spark in her eyes and the set of her chin changes my opinion. She's definitely sexy.

Who knew you had that in you, Jules?

"Because my boss told me even though I was fired for being late, if I deliver these packages, he'll pay me through the rest of the week."

"Ah." I nod and purse my lips, already making a mental note to check with Barney in the mail room to see why he fired her. Jules pulls the hem of her sweater down on her hips and, of course, it makes the V of her cleavage that much deeper.

You're just not someone who notices a girl like me

Her words ring though my mind and pull it back to what she said before the elevator moving interrupted us. "You said I'm forced to notice you. What's that supposed to mean?"

She holds my gaze for a second before shaking her head and averting her eyes down only to notice that when she fell forward, her knee crushed a box and the contents have spilled out on the floor.

Lacy things. Thong underwear in an assorted array of colors. Bikini briefs made of lace. Boy shorts in sexy satin. Each piece with the Garters & Lace logo stitched on them. Every one of them I immediately imagine her wearing beneath that sweater of hers.

Can you blame me?

Her laugh fills the car for the first time but it's not exactly warm. "Exactly," she says with a nod. "Fifteenth floor."

"C'mon, Jules. What in the hell does that mean?"

"It means that you're from the fifteenth floor. One of the

guys with the condescending smirks and the grabby hands that happen when no one is looking. You're the executive who pays no more attention to the girl from the mail room than he does the shit he sells. Shit that only fits the eye-candy he wears on his arm instead of fitting the everyday woman who would kill to feel sexy like that for a single moment. That's what I mean by the fifteenth floor." She nods resolutely like I have a fucking clue what she's talking about when I don't before looking back down and gathering the scattered panties.

I fight the square of my shoulders at her words. At her observations. At everything I haven't noticed over the past eight months since my grandfather unexpectedly died because I've been so busy taking the crash course in learning how to run this place.

Christmas bonuses not being paid to all our employees. Sexual harassment by the executives. Christ. More things I need to look into. More ways I need to bring Garters & Lace up to speed from my grandfather's antiquated ways.

And at the same time though . . . I remember the chill of the mail room. The miserable hours and unappreciated work. The dismissive attitude of the top floors toward those who work the bottom floors. The crappy food that was months past its expiration in the vending machines.

I might be running things now, but Gramps made me learn this place from the ground up.

"So what floor are you on, huh?" Jules asks and pulls me from my thoughts.

"I don't work here at Garters & Lace." The lie rolls off my tongue and I don't regret it one bit.

"Ha. Yes, you do. I've seen you strutting in here before."

"Strutting?" I laugh. "I don't strut."

She just twists her lips as she stares at me, her eyes telling me I do, the ghost of a smile on her lips reinforcing it.

"Yes, you do. I bet you strut right up to the top floor." She raises her eyebrows and sighs before looking back down to the package in her hand.

"No, seriously." I grasp for an excuse, anything to have her look at me again. "Just dropping off a marketing plan."

"For what?"

"The new fall line." She looks at me, those eyes electrifying, and I can see the moment she buys it. "What did you mean about *the shit they sell?*"

Another snort. "See? I told you, you were the problem."

This woman. She's confusing as fuck and I need a damn roadmap to follow her but hell if I don't want to take the ride while we're stuck here in the elevator.

"Come again?" I ask.

"Yes. *You.*" She shakes her head. "You may not work here but you push the shit they—Garters & Lace—sells. What about selling something to women that makes them feel good? These"—she shoves the handful of panties toward me —"only fit size zeros. They're sexy and pretty and dainty. Do you actually think they'd fit a body like mine?"

I take one from her and hold the red lace thong from the tip of my forefinger. Our eyes meet over the top of it and I can't help the smirk that plays with the corner of my lips. "We've got time. You could always try it on?" I lift an eyebrow and get a scowl from her.

Brilliant, Archer. You worry about sexual harassment of employees and then you just up and say that.

Ah, but she's not an employee anymore.

At least there's that.

That and the image of her in these sexy panties.

"That's exactly what I'm talking about. These fit models and teenagers. The ones you sell to everyday women—the norm of America that's a size fourteen to sixteen—are ridiculous. Pussy cats on underwear. Donuts on panties.

out about getting it fixed. The shop was deserted but for the shopkeeper, a knowledgeable and talkative old-timer with watery eyes. He was from a different world than Malcolm. He told me he had played in a Military Band, and had travelled the world with the Army, listing countries which retained, for him, their Empire names: Ceylon, Rhodesia, British Somaliland. He had met his wife when he was stationed in Egypt, a French dancer, and his eyes lit up as if he had met her yesterday. His reminiscences took him further and further into the past. He had done two paper rounds as a boy to save up for his first instrument. By the time he had finished, I wasn't sure if he said he had played the clarinet for 60 years, or had not played it for 60 years.

He tried to interest me in a 1969 Boosey & Hawkes 10/10 instrument, which he described with the reverence that a classic car fanatic reserves for an E-type Jaguar. Then he added that Yamaha produced an excellent new instrument for less than £1,000. Finally, when I told him my budget, he gave me his printed list, faded, copied and re-copied several times, listing repairers and teachers. And at the bottom, there was a somewhat ungrammatical NB: "Please note the Andante Music Shop is not commercially involved or responsible for this List."

He must have seen my eye on that, because he said, as if I was accusing him:

"I don't just put anyone who comes along onto the list. They're all tried and tested. I once had someone come in and offer me money. He wanted me to recommend him, him and no-one else. I showed him the door pretty smartly, I can tell you."

And that is the truth: that is what the old man said. A different world.

Drab colors. Ill fitting." She sucks in a deep breath. "And we know what day of the week it is. We don't need to wear them on our panties as a reminder. I bet you the size zeros don't have the days of the week on them."

My laugh reverberates around the tight space. Days of the week? Donuts on fabric. "So because I'm going to the fifteenth floor, I'm the reason your panties have *pussy* cats on them?

"Of course, you would focus on that." She huffs and puts her hands on her hips from where she kneels on the floor.

"Well"—I move my head from side to side as my eyes trace her hands on the swell of her hips—"that word does catch a man's attention."

"So do the words *equal opportunity lingerie*," she asserts. "Sexy comes in all sizes." She rises to her feet and I hold my hand out to help her, surprised when she takes it. "The jerk who runs this place seems to forget that. Curves are sexy."

"They sure are," I murmur, her hand still in mine as my eyes run over hers before meeting her eyes. Her lips part, her eyes flutter . . . and fuck if I don't want to kiss her right now. Step back. Step the hell back. "I'll make sure to relay your thoughts in my marketing meetings from here on out."

I half expect her to snort at the comment, but she doesn't. Instead, our eyes hold as the tension thickens around us. As my mind already has us stripped bare and lying atop these packages.

"Jules?" I ask the question but it's for so many things and I'm not sure which one to pick.

Have lunch with me.

Come work for me.

Spend the night with me.

You're simply amazing.

3

JULES

The elevator jolts and our hands pull away and before I can think—before I even realize I just want him, the executive from the upper floors, to kiss me—the doors ding open.

I gulp in the cool air of the lobby as I turn my back to him momentarily and brace my hands on the railing to catch my breath. To find some sense of sanity that I seem to have lost from the lack of oxygen in the elevator car.

There is shuffling at my back as voices near us.

"Sorry about that, Mr.—"

"Jules," Mr. Flannel Shirt says, interrupting the maintenance worker I sense standing there. I shrug into my jacket and turn to face him. "Here are your packages." He places them in my arms.

"Thanks."

"The least I can do is help you deliver them."

"No. I'm fine." I shake my head suddenly unsteady and on unsure footing. I grab the packages tighter as if they'll ground me. "I've got them."

"You sure? I know I'm *Floor Fifteen*, but I have no problem helping." He smiles softly at his joke but it's almost as if with the doors open and the real world back around us, the gap between us is that much greater.

"I'm sure." The sooner I'm away from this—from him, from this building, from this damn day—the better. "Thanks. Thank you." I start to walk and he steps in front of me.

"Wait." He reaches out and puts my reindeer antlers on my head, his fingers lingering as he tucks an errant strand of hair behind my ear. "There. Now, you're ready to go."

The lopsided smile he gives me has things stirring in me that shouldn't stir. Has parts aching in me that shouldn't be aching.

I struggle with the need to go and the want to stay. "Um—packages. You've got yours?"

"Right here," he says and tucks his package under his arm before reaching out and placing a hand on my biceps. "Jules—"

"Thanks for trying to make me laugh," I say startled by his touch and the sudden want for more of it. "For trying to make me feel better. I . . ."

"After all that, you still hate Red Vines though. It's a pity."

His line works. I smile softly. "And you won't try Twizzlers." I take a step back to gain some distance. "Merry Christmas." I give a nod before walking off the elevator and away from him.

"Merry Christmas, Jules."

His voice carries after me and it takes every ounce of restraint I possess not to turn back and look at him.

4

JULES

"Jesus Christ, Julia. I asked you for one damn thing," Barney sneers and for a moment I think of being stuck in the elevator yesterday. The *He is the reason for the season* comment and for some reason, it makes me fight back a smile despite my current situation—standing before my ex-boss asking for my final paycheck. "I asked you to deliver those packages for me and you messed that up. You were my best girl and . . . "

"You fired me, Barney. If I was your best girl, you would have given me a second chance," I huff out and look around the stacks of mail sorted but sitting idle. The mail room is empty. Barney must have let everyone work a half day for the holiday so they could all get home for Christmas Eve before the snow starts.

"Jules." My name sounds like regret and it gives me hope that I might still have a job here.

"I'm not here to cause problems. I just want my check." I shrug.

"And I just want the mistake fixed. You do realize that you

delivered the wrong package to the owner of the company, right?"

"No, I didn't. I didn't have any packages to a McMasters." I know I didn't. I've never even been to the floor his office is on.

"You say that and yet I got a call from Archer McMasters himself asking why he received a package for someone else and not the very important package he was waiting for. You think that makes me look like I run a tight ship? You think—"

"What's your point, Barney?" I ask. "You want me to switch it out? Fine. Give me my job back and I'll fix the problem. Although, I know for a fact I didn't mess anything up yesterday."

My words stop his rant and for the first time since stepping foot in here, I notice the bags under his eyes are darker, his hair a little bit messier, but there is a ghost of a smile on his lips that makes me feel like I've been played. "What?" he barks out a laugh.

"It's Christmas Eve. I'm sure you have a family to get home to when I don't have any plans . . . so go ahead and give it to me. I'll make it right."

"I was ready to bribe you to fix the problem and you just up and offer to?"

"*Shit*. Can I take the offer back then so I can hear the bribe?" I laugh, suddenly having the feeling that things might just work out. Suddenly wanting them to.

"No. You can't . . . but, you'll have my undying appreciation . . . and a little more understanding next time."

"Next time?" Hope bubbles up.

"Yes. Next time." His smile is soft and sincere. "You called and let me know about the accident and that you were going to be late. . . . I took my stress out on you."

"You did."

Our eyes hold as regret flashes through his. "I'm sorry, Jules. I overreacted."

"Thank you. Do you have the package so I can run it upstairs?" I ask.

He reaches out and hands a parcel to me. "Not upstairs. Mr. McMasters is gone for rest of the week. Let's see where it needs to go . . ." He looks down to his clipboard scribbled with a bunch of notes. "This needs to go to Tavern on the Green."

"Of course it does." I laugh because it's all I can do. The one place I wanted Alex to take me on Christmas Eve, and I'm going to end up going there simply as a mail girl delivering a package. *Perfect*.

"Your check, Jules." Barney places my check on top of the package as he slides it across the counter. "And we'll see you back here next week, same hours, same schedule."

"Really?"

"Really. Merry Christmas, Jules."

"Merry Christmas, Barney."

The subway uptown is a nightmare. Last minute shoppers pack into the car and the buzz of excitement is as prevalent in the air as the crisp coldness that owns it.

Pulling my coat tightly around me, I take my time walking through Central Park. I listen to the noises of the city at my back and watch the first few flakes of snow flit down as the door to the restaurant is opened for me.

It's just like I imagined it would look like inside—like an explosion of Christmas decorations. Trees decorated to the hilt and décor strewn about all mixed with the rich scent of food and the low hum of talking.

The host smiles at me despite the fact that I'm nowhere near dressed nicely enough to be eating here on tonight of all nights.

"Welcome to Tavern on the Green. How may I help you?"

"Hi." I pull the package out from beneath my coat where I was protecting it from the weather. "I have to deliver a package to a guest, Archer McMasters."

"Ah, yes. Ms. Jilliland? He did tell me you'd be coming. Right this way."

I nod and follow behind him, my eyes taking in everything around me. Hoping to catch a glimpse of a famous face because I've convinced myself that celebrities come here, but don't see any.

The host turns a corner to a small room where a table sits by itself near a crackling fireplace. A small Christmas tree is in the corner, the silver bulbs reflecting the flames. Two chairs sit at the table. One empty. One occupied, the back of a man to me.

"Mr. McMasters?"

"Hmm?"

"Ms. Jilliland for you."

"Great. Lovely."

And that voice.

I know that voice.

My feet freeze in place as I realize who it is.

And when Archer McMasters turns to face me, I'm met with his vibrant blue eyes behind black framed lenses. "*Ms. Jilliland.*"

Archer McMasters was the man in the elevator. The CEO of Garters & Lace. The man I told he basically didn't know how to market his own company.

Jesus.

I hate the jolt of electricity that runs through me when our eyes meet.

Seriously?

I thought I'd imagined the chemistry I felt in the elevator yesterday. I'd talked myself into believe it was nothing. But I was wrong. Oh so wrong. Because it's back with just a simple look and the sound of his voice saying my name.

I want to shrink into nothing.

Not only did I insult him, but I proved my incompetence by delivering the wrong package to him.

Kill me now.

So many thoughts run through my mind but all I can think of is if I just got my job back, I'm surely fired now.

Act professional, Jules. Give him his package and leave. Save face.

"Take a seat, Jules." His voice is low but I hear every syllable over the hum of the restaurant at my back.

"No. I—uh—your package." I take a step forward and shove it at him. "It got mixed up yesterday. I apologize. I'm sure it was important and I was flustered and I'm sorry." Every word I utter comes out faster than the last as he just sits there with those eyes of his locked on mine, his face impassive.

Archer reaches out and takes the parcel from me and sets it on the table in front of him. He points to the chair beside him but doesn't speak.

"No. I . . . again, sorry."

"Sit," he demands and I exhale audibly.

Crap. Crap. Crap.

But I oblige. And, of course, the only chair to sit in is adjacent to the corner where his is.

I try not to notice the details about him but fail. *Miserably.* The crisp, white dress shirt that is unbuttoned at the throat. The cuff links. The way his thumb runs up and down the edge of his highball glass.

"What? No reindeer antlers?" he asks.

"No." My voice is soft as I suddenly feel self-conscious in my Docs and my secondhand dress in this upscale restaurant. I smooth it down over my knees and shift in my seat.

"I like them on you."

I offer a partial smile but avert my eyes to the glass of champagne that a server just slid in front of me. "I'm sorry, you have company coming. I'll be going."

When I go to stand, Archer puts his hand on my arm and holds me still. "The package didn't get mixed up, Jules."

My head startles. "Yes, it did." I point to the label on the front. "Your name is right here. I messed up," I confess though I know I did not have a single package for Archer McMasters yesterday.

I freeze when he leans closer and the subtle scent of his cologne fills my nose. "Jules." His voice is low, the heat of his breath hits my cheek. "I did it on purpose."

I twist my face toward his, which is only inches from my own. My breath hitches and my heart races because yes, I screwed up but hell if every part of me didn't just react to all parts of him. "You what?" I ask although I know I heard him correctly.

"I wanted to see you again."

If I thought my pulse was racing moments before, my heart just flip-flopped in my chest. "Why?" My voice is barely audible.

"Several reasons." He reaches out and tucks a wayward lock of hair behind my ear, a gesture that seems so natural and intimate. When he's done, he runs the back of his hand along the line of my jaw and I fight the innate want to turn my cheek into his hand.

Desire streaks through me like I've never experienced before but with it is an anxious edge. A sharp awareness of who he is and who I am and why in the world I'm sitting here with him.

My eyes flicker to his lips and then back up to his striking blue eyes.

"Reasons?" I ask when I finally find my voice.

"Mm hmm. Reasons." His tongue darts out to lick his lips while his arm rests on the back of my chair, his thumb now running up and down the line of my spine much like it just was on his highball glass.

"And?" My voice breaks over the simple word as he turns toward me so that his knees bump mine.

"First of all, I lied to you. I'm on the twentieth floor, not the fifteenth."

"So says the label on your package."

"And I still think Red Vines are better than Twizzlers."

"Then you won't like your package. It's full of Twizzlers," I lie but melt when that soft smile slides up one corner of his mouth.

"Two can play that game." He winks.

"Noted."

"You were right."

"Naturally," I murmur and garner a laugh from him that pulls my own smile up.

"I want you to come work for me in my design department."

"What?" My voice rises in shocked pitch because that is the last thing I ever expected to fall from his mouth.

"You heard me. You were right. I went through all our products. Curves are sexy. They deserve to be celebrated— admired and adorned properly—and I know you have no problem speaking up to those on the fifteenth floor."

"Hardy-har-har."

He laughs with a shake of his head as he looks out the window where the snow is falling a little harder now.

"Equal opportunity lingerie is a thing. A really smart woman told me that."

Warmth floods through me at his comment, at the pride I feel and the disbelief still rifling through me.

"I'm serious. It's a brilliant idea and I hate that I never

thought of it. There are a lot of changes I need to make at the company . . . and I'm hoping you'll be there with me to help me make them."

"Why?"

"Because you're the only one who seems to tell me the truth. Subtlety isn't your strong suit and I need that."

"I don't even know what to say," I mutter because as much as his words have left me speechless, his fingers on the back of my neck distract me.

"Say yes, and accept this too," he says while sliding an envelope across the table toward me.

I look at him with an inquisitive smirk before grasping the envelope and opening the flap. What's inside makes me gasp aloud. It's a check payable to me for $20,000. Before I can say a word or even process what I'm looking at, Archer interjects, "You can't cash that until you say yes."

When he realizes I'm still in shock, he adds, "Jules, that's a signing bonus for the new position. One that's well deserved. And it takes care of the rent due problem the prick left you holding. There's another perk to working on the twentieth floor—corporate car service. Use it while yours is being repaired from your run in with the asshole."

I can only stare at the unexpected man sitting across from me—still trying to digest what is happening.

"Hey, Jules? One more thing."

"Hmm?"

And before I can speak, his lips meet mine in a kiss that's devastating to my senses. Every part of me sparks to life and then burns under the fire he's ignited.

When he leans back and the taste of his kiss is still on my tongue, he whispers in my ear, "I've been thinking of doing that all day."

It takes me a second to find the words that his unexpected kiss just knocked from me. "That's all you've got?"

He throws his head back and laughs loud enough that I'm sure the rest of the patrons are looking our way. "No worries there. I've got a lot more than that."

"I'm looking forward to you proving it."

He leans forward and presses a kiss so very opposite from the last one to my lips. Where before was hungry, this one is tender and soft and packed with unspoken emotions I don't even dare to think about.

"After the prick and the asshole and the shitty ice and the jerky boss," he murmurs in my ear, the heat of his breath hitting my cheek, "I think you've earned your Tavern on the Green wish. Have dinner with me."

"Archer . . . "

Yes.

Please.

"I can't. I—"

"Open the package, Julia."

"What?" His request knocks my thoughts askew.

"Open it."

I slide my finger beneath the tape and open the parcel. It's my laugh that rings out when several bags of Twizzlers spill out onto the table.

But when I look up and meet his eyes that have the fire dancing in them, my laugh falls quiet.

How did this happen?

How am I having dinner with Archer McMasters from the twentieth floor?

And why do I never want this to end.

"Merry Christmas, Jules."

"Merry Christmas, Archer."

"Is that a yes, then?" His eyes beg me more than his words do.

"Twenty thousand dollars would buy a lot of Twizzlers."

He throws his head back and laughs. "Then the offer is off the table."

He leans in and kisses me despite his words. The kind of kiss that tells me I'm wanted and desired and that this might be the start of something so unexpected but so perfectly perfect.

When I lean back and look in Archer's eyes, I know this might not be such a horrible Christmas after all.

"Yes."

ABOUT THE AUTHOR

New York Times Bestselling author K. Bromberg writes contemporary romance novels that contain a mixture of sweet, emotional, a whole lot of sexy, and a little bit of real. She likes to write strong heroines and damaged heroes who we love to hate but can't help to love.

A mom of three, she plots her novels in between school runs and soccer practices, more often than not with her laptop in tow and her mind scattered in too many different directions.

Since publishing her first book on a whim in 2013, Kristy has sold over one and a half million copies of her books across eighteen different countries and has landed on the New York Times, USA Today, and Wall Street Journal Best-sellers lists over thirty times. Her Driven trilogy (Driven, Fueled, and Crashed) is currently being adapted for film by the streaming platform, Passionflix, with the first movie (Driven) out now.

With her imagination always in overdrive, she is currently scheming, plotting, and swooning over her latest hero. You can find out more about him or chat with Kristy on any of her social media accounts.

Printed in Great Britain
by Amazon